Dear Parent:

Congratulations! Your child is taking the first steps on an exciting journey. The destination? Independent reading!

STEP INTO READING® will help your child get there. The program offers five steps to reading success. Each step includes fun stories and colorful art. There are also Step into Reading Sticker Books, Step into Reading Math Readers, Step into Reading Phonics Readers, Step into Reading Write-In Readers, and Step into Reading Phonics Boxed Sets—a complete literacy program with something to interest every child.

Learning to Read, Step by Step!

Ready to Read **Preschool–Kindergarten**
• big type and easy words • rhyme and rhythm • picture clues
For children who know the alphabet and are eager to begin reading.

Reading with Help **Preschool–Grade 1**
• basic vocabulary • short sentences • simple stories
For children who recognize familiar words and sound out new words with help.

Reading on Your Own **Grades 1–3**
• engaging characters • easy-to-follow plots • popular topics
For children who are ready to read on their own.

Reading Paragraphs **Grades 2–3**
• challenging vocabulary • short paragraphs • exciting stories
For newly independent readers who read simple sentences with confidence.

Ready for Chapters **Grades 2–4**
• chapters • longer paragraphs • full-color art
For children who want to take the plunge into chapter books but still like colorful pictures.

STEP INTO READING® is designed to give every child a successful reading experience. The grade levels are only guides. Children can progress through the steps at their own speed, developing confidence in their reading, no matter what their grade.

Remember, a lifetime love of reading starts with a single step!

To Alexis, who may be our next writer,

from Uncle David with love

—D.L.H.

Published in the United States by Random House Children's Books, a division of Random House, Inc., New York.

Visit us on the Web!
StepIntoReading.com
www.randomhouse.com/kids

Educators and librarians, for a variety of teaching tools, visit us at
www.randomhouse.com/teachers

Library of Congress Cataloging-in-Publication Data
Harrison, David L. (David Lee).
A monster is coming! / by David L. Harrison ; illustrated by Hans Wilhelm.
p. cm. — (Step into reading. A step 2 book)
Summary: When Inchworm overhears Mama Bug tell Baby Bug that she eats like a monster, he cries out in fear and sets off a chain reaction of animals trying to hide from the horrible beast they believe is coming.
ISBN 978-0-375-86677-7 (trade) — ISBN 978-0-375-96677-4 (lib. bdg.)
[1. Fear—Fiction. 2. Forest animals—Fiction. 3. Food habits—Fiction.] I. Wilhelm, Hans, ill.
II. Title.
PZ7.H2474Mon 2011
[E]—dc22 2010014513

Printed in the United States of America
10 9 8 7 6 5 4 3 2

STEP INTO READING® STEP 2

A Monster Is Coming!

by David L. Harrison
illustrated by Hans Wilhelm

Random House New York

"I'm hungry,"
said Baby Bug.

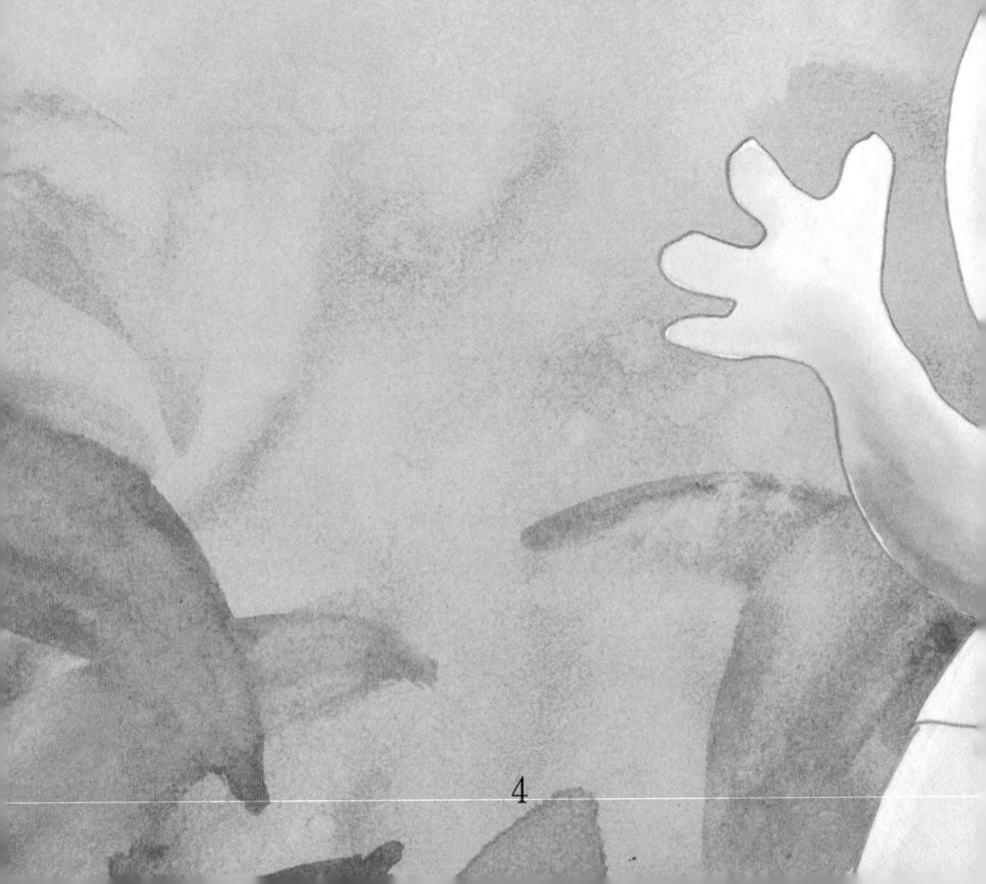

Mama Bug smiled
and gave Baby Bug
a leaf.

“You eat like a monster,”

she said.

Inchworm heard
Mama Bug say *monster*,
so he cried,
"Monster!
Inch for your lives!"

Inchworm tried to hide,

but his bottom

stuck out.

When Toad hopped by,
he said,
"Inchworm,
is that you?"

Inchworm said,
“Shhh! I’m hiding!
A monster is coming!”

"Oh no!"
said Toad.
"A horrible monster?
Leap for your lives!"

Toad tried to hide, too,

but his head stuck out.

Mouse ran by
with a mouthful of seeds.
She said,
"Toad, what are you
doing?"

"I'm hiding from
a horrible monster!"
said Toad.

"Oh my!"
said Mouse.
"A hairy, horrible
monster?
Scamper for your lives!"

Mouse tried to hide, too,

but her tail stuck out.

Rabbit tripped

on Mouse's tail.

“Oops!
Mouse, what is wrong?”
said Rabbit.

Mouse said,
"It is awful, Rabbit!
A hairy, horrible monster
is coming!"

Rabbit said,
"Oh my goodness!
A huge, hairy,
horrible monster?
Hop for your lives!"

Poor Rabbit

tried to hide,

but his ears stuck out.

Fox said,
"What is going on
around here?

Why is
everyone hiding?”

Rabbit said,
"Fox, don't you know?
A huge, hairy,
horrible monster
is coming!"

"Help me!"

yelped Fox.

"A hungry,

huge, hairy, horrible

monster is coming!"

And he dived in a hole.

Baby Bug
was chewing a leaf.
She said,
"Hey!
Why is everyone hiding?"

“A monster is coming!”
said Fox and Rabbit
and Mouse and Toad
and Inchworm. 
“Fly for your life!”

Baby Bug looked
this way and that.

She said,
"I don't see a monster,
but I'm so hungry
I could eat a monster."

Inchworm heard

Baby Bug say

eat a monster.

He shouted,

"Have you heard?

Baby Bug ate

the monster!"

"Hooray for Baby Bug!"
everyone cried.

Baby Bug was glad
she was a hero.
But talk about eating
always made her hungry.
Mama Bug smiled
and gave Baby Bug
another leaf.